BLUE AND RED MAKE PURPLE

A MUSICAL JOURNEY WITH JENNIFER GASOI
ILLUSTRATED BY STEVE ADAMS

Dear Friends,

Welcome to my musical world! I invite you to travel through the pages of this book and discover all kinds of treasures. You will learn about musical styles and instruments from around the world, have the opportunity to create your own sounds, and discover more about how I write songs just for you! *Blue and Red Make Purple* invites you to express yourself, tap into your mastery and embrace your unique gifts, just like the Purple Man!

May this book inspire you on your musical journey.

Love, Jennifer

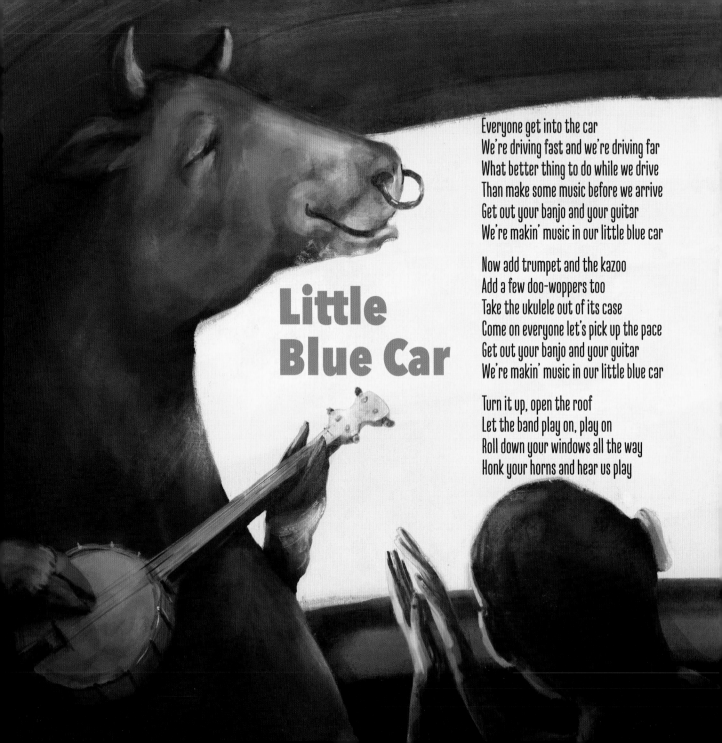

Little Blue Car

Everyone get into the car
We're driving fast and we're driving far
What better thing to do while we drive
Than make some music before we arrive
Get out your banjo and your guitar
We're makin' music in our little blue car

Now add trumpet and the kazoo
Add a few doo-woppers too
Take the ukulele out of its case
Come on everyone let's pick up the pace
Get out your banjo and your guitar
We're makin' music in our little blue car

Turn it up, open the roof
Let the band play on, play on
Roll down your windows all the way
Honk your horns and hear us play

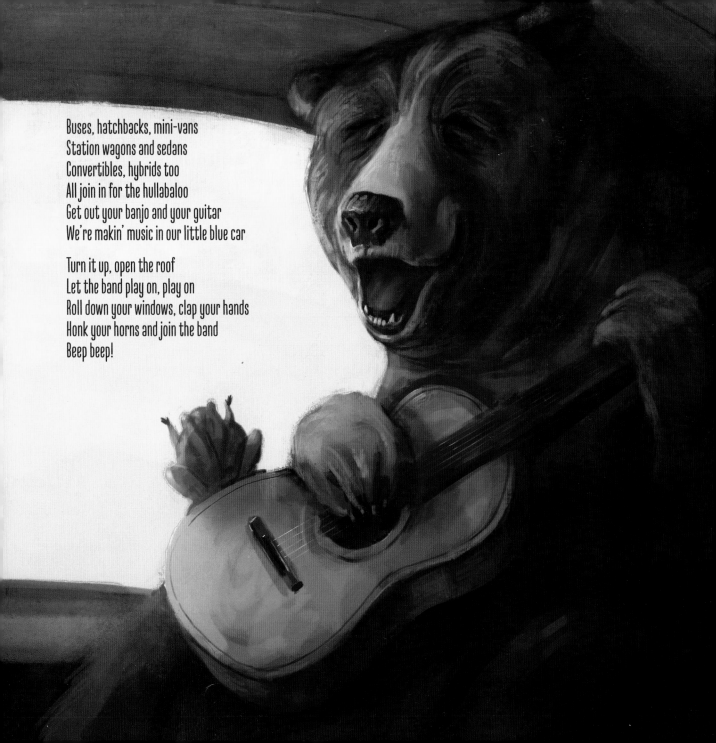

Buses, hatchbacks, mini-vans
Station wagons and sedans
Convertibles, hybrids too
All join in for the hullabaloo
Get out your banjo and your guitar
We're makin' music in our little blue car

Turn it up, open the roof
Let the band play on, play on
Roll down your windows, clap your hands
Honk your horns and join the band
Beep beep!

Throw a Penny in the Wishing Well

Find a penny in your pocket
And throw it in the wishing well

I heard that dreams come true, doo doo doo doo
There's something you can do, doo doo doo doo
To make your dreams come true
Throw a Penny in the wishing well

You can polish 'em up, doo doo doo doo
Make them shiny from the bottom to top, doo doo doo doo
You can polish 'em up
Throw a penny in the wishing well

Take some pennies
Make them shiny and new
Throw them in the wishing well
Watch your dreams come true, ooh ooh ooh

If you have a dream, doo doo doo doo
No matter how big it seem, doo doo doo doo
If you have a dream
Throw a penny in the wishing well

Different Kind of Rhythm

Different kind of rhythm, different kind of beat
You've got your own way of moving your own feet
No one can do it just like you, no one can even try
You are your own person, you don't need a reason why
You've got your own style, you've got your own groove

You're moving and groovin' and rockin' and shakin'
you've got your own tune

You are your own person, it's the way it's gotta be
Don't let anybody tell you differently
You can paint outside the lines, just so you can see
How it feels to colour in your style and not another
You've got your own style, you've got your own groove

And you love to, love to do the things
you love to do, in your own way
And you know that, you have a certain kind
of groove when, when you play

When you're eating ice cream just the way you like
Sailing on the ocean, or riding your shiny new bike
No one can do it just like you, no one can even try
You are your own person, you don't need a reason why
You've got your own style, you've got your own groove

When you're playing hopscotch, or swimming in a lake
Jumping on a trampoline, or baking your favourite cake
No one can do it just like you, no one can even try
You're your own person, you don't need a reason why
You've got your own style, you've got your own groove

Baby Blue

Baby baby baby blue, baby baby I love you
Even when the sun don't shine I love you all the time
Baby baby baby blue, baby baby I love you
Even when the moon don't shine, I love you all the time

Even when it's grey and cloudy
Even when I'm sad and pouty
Even when the sun ain't shining through

I'll cross the mountains for you
I'll cross the desert for you
I'll take the coat off my back for you
Baby baby baby baby blue

Goin' On a Trip

Goin' on a trip to Grandpa's farm, gonna milk the cows and sleep in the barn
Goin' on a trip to Hawaii, gonna eat coconuts and climb palm trees

We can take a bus, we can take a car
A magic carpet ride, will get us far
Take a red canoe, or a private plane
A hot-air balloon, or a choo-choo train
Chugalugalugaluga chugalugalugaluga choo-choo
Chugalugalugaluga chugalugalugaluga choo-choo

Goin' on a trip to New Orleans, gonna eat jambalaya and hot red beans
Goin' on a trip to Africa, zebras and lions, roar-roar

We can take a subway, or a time machine
Jump in a bottle, and travel on the sea
Take a gondola, or a fighter plane
A parachute, or a choo-choo train
Chugalugalugaluga chugalugalugaluga choo-choo
Chugalugalugaluga chugalugalugaluga choo-choo

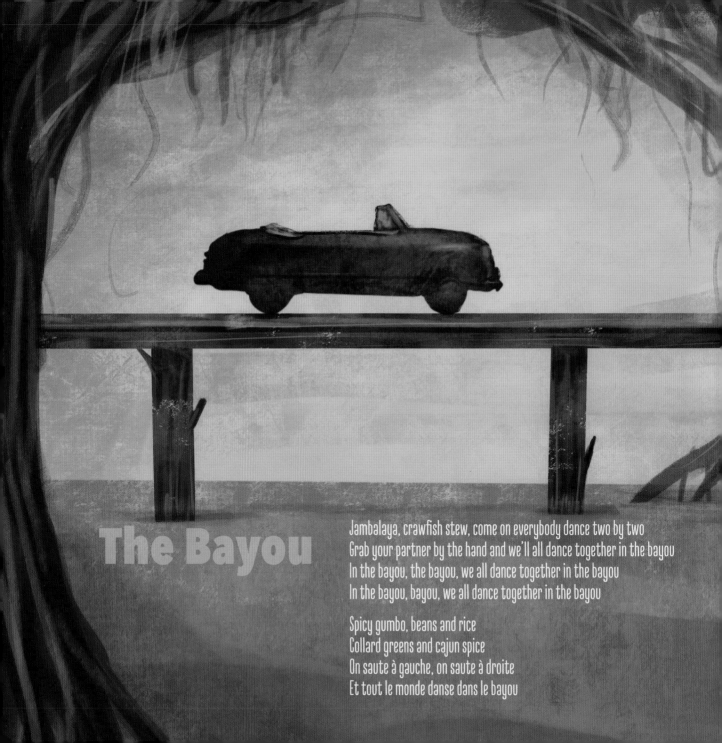

The Bayou

Jambalaya, crawfish stew, come on everybody dance two by two
Grab your partner by the hand and we'll all dance together in the bayou
In the bayou, the bayou, we all dance together in the bayou
In the bayou, bayou, we all dance together in the bayou

Spicy gumbo, beans and rice
Collard greens and cajun spice
On saute à gauche, on saute à droite
Et tout le monde danse dans le bayou

Dans le bayou, bayou, tout le monde danse dans le bayou
Dans le bayou, bayou, tout le monde danse dans le bayou

The sun is setting
Stars are coming out
Let's keep on dancing
Round and round about

Cornbread, catfish étouffée, tout le monde vient danser
Prends la main de ton ami et danse ensemble dans le bayou

Dans le bayou, bayou, we all dance together in the bayou
In the bayou, bayou, tout le monde danse dans le bayou
In the bayou, bayou, we all dance together in the bayou

The Animal Party

Look who's coming to the party, he's over there
He's brown and furry with a big black nose; it's Grizzly the bear

Look who's coming to the party, she's coming now
She's black and white with beautiful eyes; it's Candy the cow

Look who's coming to the party, with his friend the moose
He's got white feathers and a big orange beak; it's Lucky the goose

Look who's coming to the party, swingin' from a tree
He's small and cute, he plays the flute; it's Max the monkey

So come to the animal party, we'll dance the night away
There'll be milk and cake, cookies and juice, all set upon a tray
We'll howl and bark, quack and oink 'til the morning sheds her light
Nothing can stop our animal party tonight

Look who's coming to the party, hopping down the road
She's green and slimy, her color is limey; it's Betty the toad

Look who's coming to the party, all the way from the lake
He's slippery and wet, hungry I bet; it's Guido the snake

Look who's coming to the party, he's wearing a cape
He loves to climb, he's one of a kind; it's Hans the ape

Look who's coming to the party, he's wearing yellow socks
He loves to dance, he comes from France; it's George the fox

Now we're all at the party, the band starts to play
Guido and Hans, beat their drums, everyone shouts "Hurray!"
The music keeps getting faster, everyone joins their hands
Feels so right to party all night, to play our pots and pans

Didgeridoodle

I love to play, play the piano all day
I love to play, I love to play my piano all day
I love to play, play my piano all day

I love to tap dance, tap dance all day
I love to tap dance, tap tap tap all day
I love to tap dance, I love to tap dance all day

I love to sing, scat sing all day
I love to sing, I love to scat sing all day
I love to sing sing sing, I love to scat sing all day

And when I play with my band
We love to play Dixieland
I love to play with my band

I love to play, play banjo all day
I love to play, play my banjo all day
I love to play, love to play banjo all day

I love to play, didgeridoo all day
I love to play, the didgeridoodle all day
I doodle doodle doodle....
I love to play, I love to didgeridoodle all day

Hey There Joe

Hey there Joe, watcha' doing?
Planting seeds so the trees keep growin'
Red and green apples you see
Are growing on these wonderful trees

Hey there Joe, watcha' doing?
Pulling weeds so the trees'll keep growin'
Making sure the soil is fine
So the fruits will be divine

Sending love down to the roots
'Cuz these are my favourite fruits
Gotta love 'em, kiss and hug 'em
So they'll ripen under the sun

Hey there Joe, watcha' doing?
Watching rain help the trees keep on growin'
Drop by drop it trickles down
To the roots under the ground

Joe sits under the tree
Cuz it's the best place to be
Meditatin' and a waitin'
For the trees to start a bloomin'

Hey there Joe, watcha' doing?
Pickin' apples before it starts snowin'
Round and ripe shiny and new
Here is one just for you
Round and ripe shiny and new
Here is one just for you

Hey there Joe, watcha' doing?

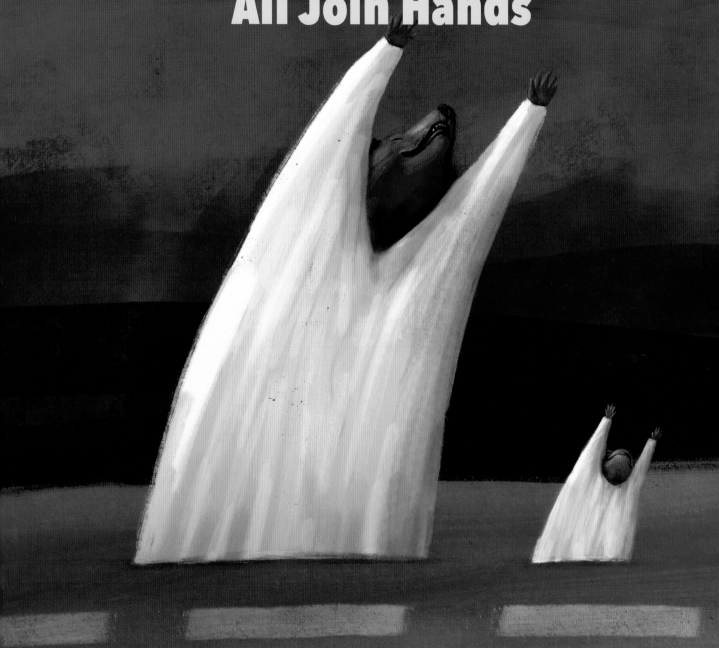

All join hands, make a circle
All join hands, for today
All join hands in celebration
For the good things coming our way

You may right, you may be wrong
You may be weak, you may be strong
But no matter what's goin' on
If we just join hands, we'll get along

For the good things comin' our way
For the love here today
For the good life here today
All join hands, here today!

Bright Side of Life

When you're feeling sad and lonely, and you don't know what to do
Instead of bright and sunny, the world looks awfully blue
And you know that things will get better, you have nothing to fear
If you sit in the rain long enough, a rainbow will appear

And you've got to have heart, you've got to have hope
If you don't look at the bright side of life, how are you gonna cope?
There are so many places to go, so many things to do
I'm gonna look on the bright side of life, how 'bout you?

When the sky is grey and cloudy, and the rain's fallin' on your head
And all you want to do today is go right back to bed
Remember all the good things, the things that make you smile
The sun will be shining again in a little while

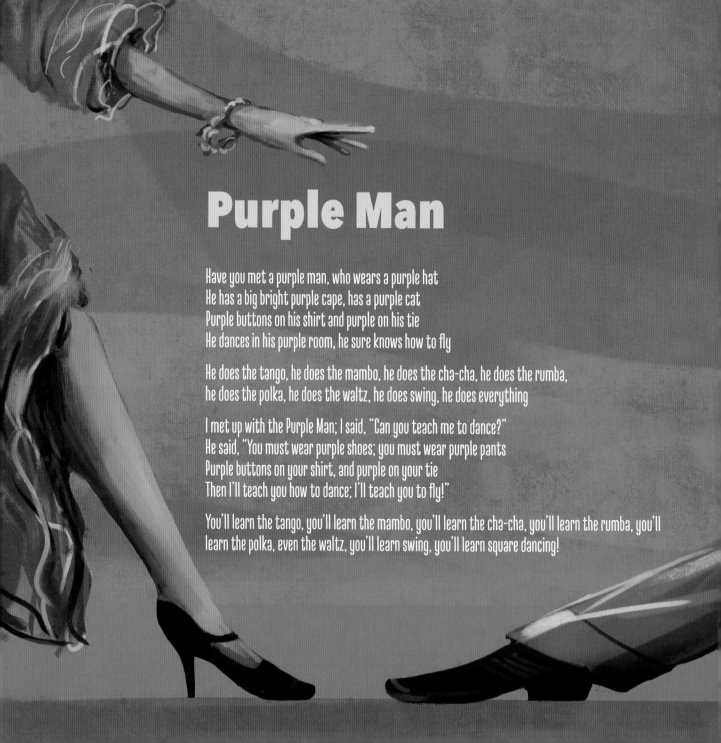

Purple Man

Have you met a purple man, who wears a purple hat
He has a big bright purple cape, has a purple cat
Purple buttons on his shirt and purple on his tie
He dances in his purple room, he sure knows how to fly

He does the tango, he does the mambo, he does the cha-cha, he does the rumba,
he does the polka, he does the waltz, he does swing, he does everything

I met up with the Purple Man; I said, "Can you teach me to dance?"
He said, "You must wear purple shoes; you must wear purple pants
Purple buttons on your shirt, and purple on your tie
Then I'll teach you how to dance; I'll teach you to fly!"

You'll learn the tango, you'll learn the mambo, you'll learn the cha-cha, you'll learn the rumba, you'll
learn the polka, even the waltz, you'll learn swing, you'll learn square dancing!

Swing your partner round and round and round and round and round she goes
Swing your partner round and round and round and round she goes
Alaman left and a dosey dosey dosey dosey dosey doe
Swing your partner round and round and round and round she goes

I began to dance around, dancing to the beat
With a purple hat upon my head, purple shoes upon my feet
I danced and danced in a purple room upon a purple floor
I danced and danced the whole night long, I'll dance forever more

I do the tango, I do the mambo, I do the cha cha-cha-cha, I do the rumba, I do the polka,
I do the waltz, I do swing, I do square dancing

Listening guide

The answers to the questions in red can be found at the end of this section.

Jamming with the band

Little Blue Car

BLUEGRASS • TRACK 1

Everyone jump in our little blue car and join the band for a bluegrass jamboree! Bluegrass is a form of American roots music related to folk and country, with elements of jazz. It is a popular kind of music throughout the Appalachian Mountains and in the areas of Kentucky, Tennessee, Virginia, Maryland and North Carolina. "Bluegrass" refers to a smooth meadow-grass found in Kentucky. A bluegrass band consists of a "rhythm section," a group of musicians who form the foundation for the song. In "Little Blue Car," the rhythm section is made up of piano, guitar, banjo, upright bass and drums.

"Little Blue Car" is no ordinary bluegrass song! It is full of unexpected sounds, instruments and surprises that make it unique. For starters, there are kazoos, doo-woppers (you will learn about doo-wop in the next song) and improvised trumpet sounds that I made myself! (at 0:50) I used my mouth to simulate the sound of a trumpet and made up melodies on the spot. Making up music on the spot is called improvisation. I recorded three different trumpet parts to make it sound like there was a whole band of trumpets! Can you make trumpet sounds with your mouth and play along with me?

Johnny Star, the radio announcer, makes an appearance in the middle of the song. During his announcement for "Wishing Well Radio," you will hear a jingle, which is a short, catchy tune often used in commercials (at 1:44). ❶ What four-letter word does the jingle spell? You can create and sing your own jingle using your name or favourite word! Johnny talks about a "jam" happening on the expressway. He's talking about a musical jam, not the kind of jam you put on your toast! A musical jam happens when lots of musicians get together and play music. Would you like to jam with my band and me? It's easy! Grab your favourite instrument, turn on the music, and play along with us!

Having fun playing with words

Throw a Penny in the Wishing Well

DOO-WOP • TRACK 2

The inspiration for "Throw a Penny in the Wishing Well" is doo-wop, a 1950's style of music that originated out of the African-American communities in the United States. Some of the most popular doo-wop groups include The Chordettes ("Lollipop"), The Platters ("Great Pretender") and The Silhouettes ("Get a Job"). Doo-wop is made up of close vocal harmonies and nonsense words and phrases sung in a certain rhythm. The first nonsense phrase in the song is "doo doo doo doo". ❶ How many times do you hear this phrase in the song? ❷ Can you find the "wa-ooh wa wa wa-ooh" sections? The final nonsense phrase "ooh sh-bop, ooh ooh sh-bop" can be found in the middle of the song (at 1:06). Can you clap the rhythms of these phrases? For an added challenge, can you clap and sing the phrases at the same time? Now can you clap, sing and ride a unicycle while eating jellybeans at the same time?

Doo-wop music is characterized by a rhythm section with a strong lead vocalist—which is another word for "singer." In this song the rhythm section consists of piano, guitar, upright bass and drums. To add a little flavour and fun to the music, a horn player plays a solo in the middle of the song. He plays on top of the "ooh sh-bops." ❸ Can you identify what kind of horn is playing the solo? Another example of a doo-wop song that also has the same instrument playing a solo is "Yakkity Yak" by the Coasters.

Now that you have an idea of what nonsense phrases sound like, you can create your own!
Zoo-bee doo-bee, eeby-deeby, heeby jeeby da-doo run-run. Playing with words is much fun!

Being you in all that you do

Different Kind of Rhythm

BLUES • TRACK 3

This is a song written in a style of music called the blues. Blues was developed by African-Americans in the "deep South" of the United States in the late 1800s. It's the kind of music that allows people to express sadness and emotion during hard times. One of the most famous blues singers and guitarists of all time is a musician named B.B. King. Also known as the "King of Blues," B.B. King played shows until he was 87 years old! There are many types of blues from different regions. Each has its own unique flavor. For example, swamp blues comes from areas in the U.S. that have swamps, such as Louisiana. Do you know what reptile lives in swamps? It's green, has sharp teeth and rhymes with Darth Vader. Yes! An Alligator! Other kinds of blues include boogie-woogie, rhythm and blues, Mississippi Delta blues, country blues, and Memphis blues.

Not all blues songs are sad. "Different Kind of Rhythm" is actually a happy song that doesn't have the typical blues sadness. That's the beauty of writing music. You get to make up your own rules! And actually, that's what this song is about: being yourself, doing things your own way and expressing your unique voice. In blues songs, a musician will often express his or her unique voice by taking a solo. A solo is when the vocalist stops singing and one of the instrumentalists has a moment to shine. ❶ Can you find the solo in this song? ❷ Can you name the instrument that plays the solo?

You can write your own blues songs about all kinds of subjects! Here are a few ideas for blues songs: "My dog ate my favorite shoes blues," or "My mom won't let me eat candy for dinner blues." Or you could write a happier blues song such as "I'm too happy to write the blues blues." Anything goes when you let the ideas flow!

Baby Blue

FOLK • TRACK 4

"Baby Blue" is inspired by a genre (style) of music called folk. A few celebrated folk musicians include Bob Dylan ("Blowin' in the Wind"), Woody Guthry ("This Land is Your Land"), Pete Seeger ("Green Grass Grows All Around") and Joni Mitchell ("Circle Game"). Folk music features stringed instruments that may include guitar, banjo or ukulele, and a wind instrument such as a harmonica. In traditional folk music, the singer tells a story with a theme such as peace, freedom or love. ❶ Can you identify the theme of "Baby Blue"?

Two instruments play together at the beginning of the song. One of the instruments looks like a small guitar with only four strings. It is popular in Hawaii. ❷ Do you know what it's called? The instrument that plays along with this string instrument has a similar sound to that of a harmonica or accordion. It's called a melodica. It's sometimes referred to as a "wind piano" because it is played like a horn using the breath while played like a piano using the fingers on a keyboard.

I love making up rhymes in my songs. ❸ See if you can complete these rhymes. Baby Blue I love ___. Even when the sun don't shine, I love you all the ___. Can you find some other words that rhyme with each other? How about a word that rhymes with snow? Or dog? How about star? If you can rhyme with these words, you are on your way to writing music!

So grab your ukulele, let's sing a tune, we'll write some songs under the moon!

Choosing notes that sound like words
Goin' On a Trip
JAZZ • TRACK 5

I love to travel, I love trains, and I love jazz! I put them all together to write "Goin' On a Trip." Jazz music is played by a rhythm section which often includes piano, guitar, bass and drums. Different instruments like trumpets, saxophones, and even fiddles may join the rhythm section. For our first stop to Grandpa's farm, we add a dash of the fiddle to create the feeling of being in the country. Next, we travel to one of my favorite places in the world... Hawaii! Can you hear the sound of coconuts (at 0:41)? You can make a coconut sound by tapping your cheeks with your hands and making an "oh" shape with your mouth! Can you hear how the piano part sounds like we're climbing trees (at 0:46)? There is also a musical reference to a fun jazz song called "Salt Peanuts" written by a famous trumpet player named Dizzie Gillespie (at 0:56). Say "salt peanuts, salt peanuts" out loud, and see if you can find the piano notes that sound like these words. It's a little tricky but I know you can do it!

In the next part of the song, I sing about the different ways we can travel. ❶ Can you name a few modes of transportation that I mention? During this section, the guitar plays lots of improvised melodies. Do you remember what improvisation is? Just in case you need a reminder, it's when musicians make up melodies and music on the spot. It is one of the most important elements in jazz music. Throughout this song, we create the sound effect of a train whistle using a specific instrument. ❷ Can you identify which instrument this is? I'll give you a "widdle" hint... we heard it when we visited Grandpa's farm.

If you could go anywhere in the world where would you go? How would you get there? The sky's the limit when you use your imagination! Who knows, maybe we'll meet each other on our magic carpets on our way to the moon!

The Bayou

The Cajun style of music is the inspiration for the song "The Bayou." The roots of Cajun music come from the French-speaking Acadians of Canada who settled in the Maritimes and parts of Quebec in the 1700s. In 1765, Acadians began migrating to Louisiana, and a vibrant Creole culture of music, dance and delicious food was born. When you listen to the lyrics of "The Bayou," you will discover all kinds of these foods. Crawfish is seafood that comes from the bayou—a marshy lake or wetland found in Southern states like Louisiana and Texas. ❶ Can you name some of the other Cajun foods you hear in this song?

Like Cajun spice which combines spices like cumin, coriander, paprika and cayenne, Cajun music has a particular blend of instruments that make it unique. ❷ Can you name two of the instruments that give this song a Cajun flavour? One is a string instrument and the other has a little keyboard that resembles a piano. You can hear them play solos right after the lyrics "let's keep dancing round and round about." During the bridge of the song (middle section) I sing "stars are coming out." I play an instrument called a glockenspiel that creates a star-like sound (at 1:10 after the lyrics "stars are comin' out"). It is a percussion instrument with metal plates that resemble piano keys. Cajun music also blends different languages together. ❸ Can you name the two languages you hear in this song?

Mardi Gras is a festival that takes place in New Orleans every year and is one huge party. People wear costumes and masks, eat lots of Cajun food and dance under the stars! A fun activity would be to create your own masks, cook up some jambalaya, and have a Mardi Gras celebration of your own! As they say in New Orleans, "Laissez les bons temps rouler!" (pronounced: Lay-say le bon tom roo-lay).

The Animal Party

KLEZMER • TRACK 7

"The Animal Party" is a song written in a style of music called klezmer, which originates from the Jewish people of Eastern Europe. During important celebrations, groups of musicians called klezmorim would perform klezmer songs. At Jewish weddings, one can often hear guests enjoying a famous klezmer dance song called "Hava Nagila." You will hear a sample of this song at the end of the book. Keep your ears open for it!

One of the instruments that give klezmer its distinctive sound is the clarinet. It is so playful that it almost feels like a character in the song! Can you hear the clarinetist play a solo at the beginning of the song? Listen carefully and you can hear a small excerpt of circus music played by the clarinetist during the lai lai section (at 3:07 - the title is called "Entrance of the Gladiators, Op 68"). This is called a musical reference, where a short interlude of one song is hidden within the main song. Another instrument that is popular in klezmer music is the accordion. You can hear the accordion accompany George the Fox during his dance! Now we know that the accordion is a prominent instrument in both klezmer and Cajun music. The animals in this song are pretty amazing, and some of them even play instruments! ❶ Which instrument does Max the monkey play (at 0:50)? ❷ How about Guido and Hans (at 2:47)? ❸ Which homemade kitchen percussion instruments does everyone at the party play (at 2:56)?

If I were to host an animal party, I'd invite Grizzly, Candy, Lucky, Max, Betty, Guido, Hans, George, a panda bear, a sea horse, a kangaroo, a unicorn and a cuckoo bird! Which animals would you invite to your party? Perhaps you can make your own animal puppets with pencil crayons, cardboard, glue and popsicle sticks. Then you can grab your pots and pans, play some klezmer tunes, and dance the night away!

Didgeridoodle

DIXIELAND SWING • TRACK 8

"Didgeridoodle" is a song that mixes two styles of jazz music together: swing and Dixieland. Swing music was developed in America in the 1930s. Some of the best-known bandleaders of the swing era were Duke Ellington ("Take the A-Train"), Count Basie ("Basie Boogie") and Glenn Miller ("In the Mood"). One of my favorite singers of all time, Ella Fitzgerald, often sang with these big bands. Known as the "Queen of Jazz," Ella was a master of scat singing, a technique where singers use their voice as an instrument and invent melodies using nonsensical words. ❶ Can you find the part of the song where I scat? Dixieland is a style of jazz that was developed in New Orleans in the early 1900s. Have you ever heard of the song "When the Saints go Marching In"? This is a famous Dixieland song! In the middle of the song, you will hear the "Didgeridoodle" Dixieland band play. ❷ Which horn instruments do you hear?

Just for fun, I added an instrument in this song that is not typically associated with swing or jazz. In fact, it comes from a country that is famous for kangaroos, koalas, and kiwifruit! Can you guess which country it is? Yes! It's Australia! The most famous instrument in Australia is called the didgeridoo. Do you remember how I made the sound of a trumpet in "Little Blue Car"? I do something similar here. Instead of using a real didgeridoo, I create a didgeridoo effect by making an "ooh" shape with my mouth while singing "you you you you you you" really fast. Go ahead and make the sound! I can almost guarantee you will start laughing!

Grab your pianos and tap shoes, your didgeridoos,
Let's put on a show for the kangaroos!
With banjos and trumpets, trombones in hand,
Let's travel to Australia with our Dixieland band!

Hey There Joe

ROOTS • TRACK 9

Joe invites us to enter his world of roots music which combines many musical styles including blues, bluegrass, old time music, jug band, country and folk. To understand this mix of styles, imagine a chocolate chip cookie. What happens if you add oatmeal, toffee, white chocolate chips and peanut butter? You end up with a whole different type of cookie! That's what happens with music. When you combine many different kinds of styles, you end up with a whole different kind of song. Since I love jazz, I added some scat singing into the mix. Do you remember when we learned about scatting in "Didgeridoodle"? All you have to do to scat is sing lots of funny sounds, like "boo-ba bee-boo, diddlee-dee." And voilà, you can scat, just like me!

There are a few elements that make this song extra special. There is a musical surprise after the lyrics "meditatin' and a waitin', for the trees to start a bloomin'." ❶ Can you name the musical style (genre) of this interlude? ❷ Which instrument plays it? A few of the most famous composers in this genre include Mozart, Beethoven, Bach and Chopin. This song is also special because it is a duet between myself and Joe (a duet means we sing together). Sometimes we talk to each other, and sometimes we sing in unison. ❸ Can you find the parts of the song where we sing in unison and the parts where we sing in harmony? Unison means we sing the same melody at the same time. Harmony means that we sing different notes at the same time.

Here's an idea for a fun activity. While listening to "Hey There Joe," draw a picture inspired by the song. You can draw yourself planting seeds in the earth, Joe meditating under a tree, or white apple blossoms blooming on a tree. Or feel free to use your imagination and draw anything that comes to mind. Maybe your apples are red, blue and purple! Or perhaps you are planting seeds that bloom into magical fruits that you've never seen before! After you've finished your drawing, you can even make the drawings come to life by dancing to the song and creating actions to the lyrics!

Bringing people together

All Join Hands

GOSPEL • TRACK 10

"All Join Hands" is a song written in a style of music called gospel. Gospel is an uplifting and inspirational genre of music that brings people together in song, dance and prayer. It is often heard in churches during religious services and celebrations. Call and response is a musical form found in gospel music. In call and response, the lead singer sings a phrase and the choir "calls back" the same or similar phrase. It is a kind of communication. ❶ Can you find the part of the song where there is call and response between myself and the choir? Can you join the choir and sing along with us?

❷ Now that you've learned all about call and response, can you name the instruments that form the rhythm section of this song? Another instrument joins the rhythm section half way through and plays a solo after the lyrics "for the good things coming our way." ❸ Do you know its name? I'll give you a hint. If you take the letter after A, the number after 2 and put the word organ afterwards, you get the name! Right after the solo, something happens... the instruments disappear! Instead of playing their instruments, the whole band claps their hands and sings with the choir. Only one percussion instrument still plays. It looks like a wooden circle with small metal discs around the edges. Do you know what it's called? Its name sounds like the word tangerine. If you guessed tambourine, you are a superstar!

Here's a fun activity you can do with your friends or family. Make a circle and invite one person to dance in the middle. Then do the same dance move together. Keep going until everyone has had a chance to dance in the center. Then open up the circle, turn up the music and keep on dancing!

Bright Side of Life

CALYPSO • TRACK 11

This bright, sunny song is in a style of Afro-Caribbean music called calypso that has origins in Venezuela, Trinidad, Tobago and West Africa. In the 1950s, a Caribbean-American singer named Harry Belafonte, also known as "The King of Calypso," made calypso music popular all over the world. One of his most well-known songs is called "Day-O (The Banana Boat Song)." Calypso is an upbeat, fun, danceable kind of music that often features guitar, congas, bongos, steel pan drums, maracas, clavés, trumpets and trombones. In "Bright Side of Life," there are four main instruments. ❶ Can you identify them? ❷ Which string instrument is featured at the beginning of the song? ❸ Can you find the section of the song where I scat? As you may have noticed, I love to scat!

I also love to put little surprises into my songs. After the lyrics "and the rain's falling on your head," there is a sound that I created by dropping a pebble into a glass of water (at 0:56). Take a moment to listen closely. Can you hear it? Can you think of other fun ways to create sound? Here's one idea. You can make your own maracas out of toilet paper rolls, pebbles, rice or lentils and decorate them with colourful art! You can play, shake and dance to the music using your very own percussion instruments.

Now you're ready to have a calypso party!

Exploring a kaleidoscope of musical genres

Purple Man

VARIOUS MUSICAL STYLES • TRACK 12

What colour do you get when you mix blue and red together? Purple! What song do you get when you mix tango, mambo, cha-cha, rumba, polka, waltz, swing, square dancing and the hora? The Purple Man! Yes, this song takes us on a madcap whirlwind tour of musical influences and genres from all around the world!

The cha-cha, mambo and rumba are all dances that come from Cuba. ❶ Do you know which horn instrument is popular in Cuba? You can hear it play a solo at the beginning of the song and two more solos in the middle (at 0:57 and 2:08). During the square dance, you will hear an instrument that was featured in "Goin' on a Trip." ❷ Do you remember what it's called? And at the very end of the song, we hear a sample of "Hava Nagila" which is a song in the style of klezmer. It is played during a Jewish dance called the hora. ❸ Can you recall which song in the book is also in the style of klezmer? If you have forgotten, maybe Guido, Hans or Max can remind you! We learned that one of the most important instruments in klezmer music is the clarinet. You can hear the clarinet play with the band during the hora. There's so much going on; you'll have to listen closely!

The Purple Man is someone who is passionate about two things in life: the colour purple and dancing! What are you passionate about in your life? What do you love to do? One of my passions is writing music for you! I also love dogs, (especially Shelties) Thai food, swimming in the ocean, dancing, drinking coconut water from real coconuts, and finding rocks and crystals. I encourage you all to discover your passions in life and follow your dreams. Maybe I'll see you traveling to Hawaii in your hot-air balloon, jamming with Johnny Star in your little blue car, or dancing the cha-cha in Cuba with the Purple Man! No matter where you go, or what you do, follow your heart and always be you!

Answers

Little Blue Car TRACK 1

① The four-letter word is D-R-O-P

Throw a Penny in the Wishing Well TRACK 2

① The "doo doo doo" phase is sung 8 times

② "Wa-ooh wa wa wa-ooh" sections at 0:38 and 1:31

③ The saxophone plays the solo

Different Kind of Rhythm TRACK 3

① The solo plays at 1:30 after the chorus "Movin' and Groovin'…"

② The instrument that plays the solo is the piano

Baby Blue TRACK 4

① The theme of "Baby Blue" is love

② The instrument that plays with the melodica is the ukulele

③ The words that complete the rhymes are "you" and "time"

Goin' on a Trip TRACK 5

① The modes of transportation are bus, car, magic carpet, red canoe, privateplane, hot-air balloon, choo-choo train (at 1:07) Subway, time machine, jump in a bottle and travel on the sea, gondola, fighter plane, parachute (at 2:57)

② The fiddle makes the sound of a train whistle

The Bayou TRACK 6

① Cajun foods in the song include jambalaya, beans and rice, crawfish stew, collard greens, cornbread, catfish, étouffée

② The two instruments are violin and accordion

③ The two languages are English and French

The Animal Party TRACK 7

1. Max the monkey plays the flute
2. Guido and Hans beat their drums
3. The homemade instruments are pots and pans

Didgeridoodle TRACK 8

1. I scat at 1:18
2. The horn instruments in the Dixieland band include trumpet, muted trumpet and clarinet

Hey There Joe TRACK 9

1. The genre is classical music at 1:44
2. The piano plays the interlude
3. We sing in unison at:
   1:27 "ba ba ba"
   2:07 "round and ripe shiny and new"

   We sing in harmony at:
   0:49 "so they'll ripen under the sun"
   2:12 "just for you"

All Join Hands TRACK 10

1. The call and response section starts at 0:49
2. The rhythm section includes piano, guitar, upright bass and drums
3. The instrument is a B3 organ

Bright Side of Life
TRACK 11

1. The four main instruments are piano, guitar, upright bass and drums
2. The guitar is featured at the beginning of the song
3. I scat at 1:38

Purple Man TRACK 12

1. The trumpet is popular in Cuba
2. The instrument that plays during the square dance is the fiddle at 1:56 and 2:59
3. "The Animal Party" is in the style of klezmer

All songs written, arranged and produced by **Jennifer Gasoi**
Recorded and mixed by **Pierre Messier** at Studio Piccolo (except *Hey There Joe* vocals recorded by Miles Hill at Frequency Studio)
Mastered by **Peter Moore** at The E-Room Artistic Director **Roland Stringer** Illustrations **Steve Adams**
Graphic design **Stéphan Lorti** for Haus Design Copy editing **Ruth Joseph**

MUSICIANS

Jennifer Gasoi lead vocals, harmonies, trumpet vocalize, ukulele, melodica, glockenspiel, piano (*Bright Side of Life*)
John Sadowy piano, B3 organ, percussion, backup vocals, radio voice of "Johnny Star"
Andy Dacoulis guitar **Gilbert Joanis** bass **Richard Irwin** drums **Ron Dilauro** trumpet **Christopher Smith** tuba
Jonathan Moorman fiddle **Pierre Messier** accordion **Michael Jerome Brown** banjo (*Little Blue Car*)
Patrick Vetter saxophone, clarinet, vocals (*Purple Man*) **Eric Bibb** vocals (*Hey There Joe*)
Alan Prater and **Jewelle Mackenzie** backup vocals (*Different Kind of Rhythm* and *All Join Hands*)
Sam Harrisson drums (*Didgiridoodle* and *Goin' on a Trip*) **Ali Labelle** piano (*Didgiridoodle* and *Goin' on a Trip*)
Yanik Cloutier banjo (*Didgiridoodle*)

Artist information available at www.jennifergasoi.com Master recordings under license from **Jennifer Gasoi**
All songs published by **Jennifer Gasoi Publishing** administered by **Hyvecity Music Inc.**

Steve Adams dedicates this album to his daughter **Elisabeth**, a radiant and inspirational person

ⓦ www.thesecretmountain.com
ⓒⓟ 2016 The Secret Mountain (Folle Avoine Productions)
ISBN 10: 2-924217-79-2 / ISBN 13: 978-2-924217-79-5

1087   58/863)